Brunus and the New Bear

Brunus

and the New Bear

ELLEN STOLL WALSH

Doubleday & Company, Inc., Garden City, New York

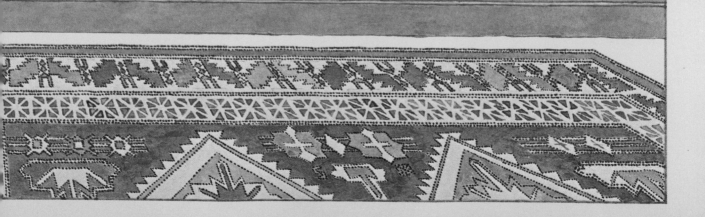

Library of Congress Catalog Card Number 78-22361
ISBN 0-385-14660-4 Trade
ISBN 0-385-14661-2 Prebound
Copyright © 1979 by Ellen Stoll Walsh

For the real Benjamin

Benjamin and Brunus were always together. They had
been friends since before they could remember. Brunus
had been given to Benjamin when Benjamin was only a
little baby.

People said that they had grown up together. Of course, Benjamin was the only one who had actually done any growing, since stuffed bears don't really grow. But that didn't matter. They were best friends.

One day while Benjamin and Brunus were playing, a
package came for Benjamin.

In it was a little bear.

Benjamin loved the new bear. He named it Heek.

Everyone admired the little bear. Benjamin felt impor-
tant. Instead of running noisily about the house as he
usually did, he walked on tiptoe and spoke in whispers.
"Heek is sleeping," he explained.

But the quiet made Brunus nervous. He did not understand why Benjamin was making so much fuss over a
bear who was too little to do anything interesting.
Benjamin did not play with Brunus for the rest of the

day. He was too busy with Heek. Poor Brunus lay on the floor where Benjamin had dropped him when the package came. Nobody even noticed. He was sad, lonely, and a little angry.

It was late when Benjamin finally thought of Brunus and carried him off to bed.

And when Benjamin put Heek in bed between them,
Brunus knew that he must do something.

Brunus waited until Benjamin was asleep. Then he gave a little shove, and bump! Heek was on the floor.

Brunus felt better. He snuggled down in the warm bed next to Benjamin.

Brunus woke up early. He wished that an eagle would whoosh down and carry Heek away. Then he thought of a plan. He would hide Heek. Benjamin would soon forget about the little bear.

Brunus was very excited. He slipped down off the bed and looked around for a hiding place.

He poked Heek under the rug . . .

and wondered if Benjamin would notice the lump.

Just then Benjamin woke up. He looked for Heek. He looked for him in the blankets and under the pillows.

He looked on the floor and under the bed.

Then he looked at Brunus. "Brunus, do you know
where Heek is?" he said.

Brunus felt ashamed. He had hoped Benjamin would
be happy that Heek was gone. He pointed to the rug.

At first Benjamin was very angry with Brunus. He wondered why he would do such a thing. But when he saw how unhappy Brunus was, he began to understand. He put his arm around his big bear and told him this story.

"Once upon a time there was a boy who had a bear. They were best friends.

Then one day another bear came to live with them.

The boy loved the new bear.

The first bear was very sad. He thought the boy didn't love him any more. But he was wrong. The boy loved him very much.

The boy hoped his two bears would be friends. Soon they were, and the three of them lived happily ever after."

Brunus thought it was a very good story.

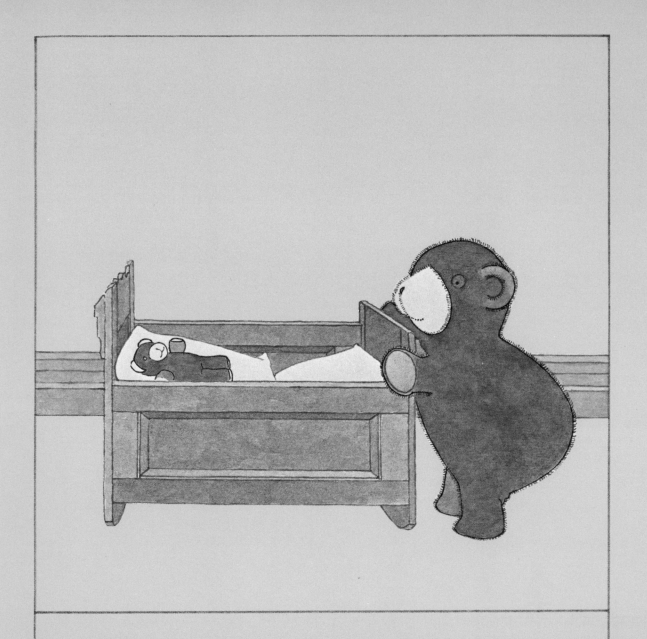

In the days that followed, Brunus did learn to love
Heek. He helped Benjamin take care of the little bear.

It is true that he sometimes tried to get Benjamin's attention away from Heek by doing silly things.

And he got a funny feeling in his tummy whenever Benjamin cuddled Heek. Sometimes, even though he knew he was a big bear, he wanted to be cuddled too.

But when Heek was sleeping, Benjamin and Brunus
would tiptoe to another part of the house . . . and play
the wonderful games they had always played.

Now when the three friends go to bed, Benjamin sleeps in the middle. "Goodnight, bears," he says.